T0132086

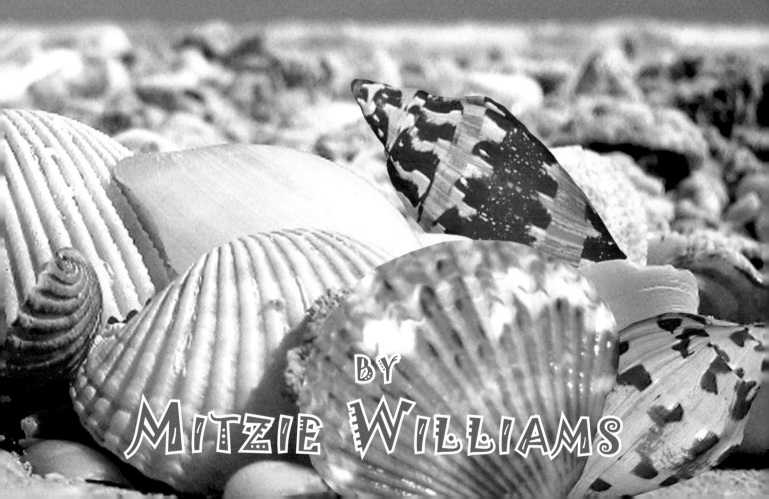

SEASHELLS

Children's Poems
and Bedtime Stories

BY
MITZIE WILLIAMS

To order additional copies of this book, contact:
Xlibris
1-888-795-4274
www.Xlibris.com
Orders@Xlibris.com, online bookstores, Jesus Book and Gift
Store, mitziewilliams89@yahoo.com

Contents

Introduction

This is a picture book of enchanting poems and incredible bedtime stories. It was divinely inspired through the Holy Spirit's prompting and instruction for each word. *Seashells* seek to enhance the listening, reading, and pronunciation skills of both the reader and listener. It also builds self-esteem and opens awareness of one's environment. Seashells are precious treasures just as children are beautiful gems, unique with different arrays of wonderful colors. I hope that *Seashells* will broaden the mind and develop good reading habits.

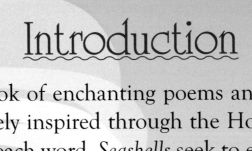

Acknowledgements

I honor the awesome power and divine authority of Jehovah, Jesus Christ, and the blessed Holy Spirit's influence to pen this creative collection of poems and bedtime stories. I thank Jesus Christ for this great wisdom, knowledge, and insight bestowed upon me as a channel to bless others with the written word.

Firstly, I want to express sincere thanks to Queen Teach and her beloved family for their outstanding kindness, love, and solid support over many years.

Secondly, I am thankful for the tremendous effort, love, and valuable contribution of Hope-Elizabeth, especially as my executive super-secretary. I would also like to mention that I appreciate the firm support of Jermit, especially his gentle understanding when I am engrossed with piles of paper everywhere.

Thirdly, I would like to give special thanks and recognition to Jason Brown who made a bold effort to request that I write children's books, especially bedtime stories.

Fourthly, I would like to give worthwhile mention to Minister Christopher Daubon and Deacon Hopeton Richards for their motivation and continued efforts to inspire the writer and poet within me. I am truly blessed by their dynamic motivation. Many thanks to all Christian brethren, supporters, acquaintances, well-wishers, friends and family; especially Joyce, sisters, brothers, cousins, nieces, nephews and relatives for their dynamic spirit and great enthusiasm.

Dedication

To my blessed offspring: Hope-Elizabeth and Jermit...

To all my special cousins, nephews and nieces especially Alicia, Ashley, Ali, and Zeke...

To all the wonderful children of the whole universe.

Seashells

Seashells, seashells, everywhere!
In plastic, trays, and jars
Hidden beneath white sand
Scattered on the land

Big seashells, tiny seashells everywhere
White, cream and brown
Hard shells, smooth shells
Everyone loves to stroll for seashells

Seashells a rare treasure
See! The ocean swells
With lobster, mussel and oyster
Tossing rings of laughter

Mitzie Williams

The White Beach

Splash! Splish! Roars the dashing waves
Upon the long shore
Dazzling with bright umbrellas
And swinging hammocks

Swash! Swish! Roars the crashing waves
Rushing upon gentle hands
Curling a jug of lemonade
Sweeping away the tiny sand castle

Mitzie Williams

The Blue Sky

See! The blue sky
Where the tiny birds flutter
And the big birds dance away
From the thick clouds

See! The airplane gliding by
With silver wings
Waving down at me
Like a lost bird

Mitzie Williams

The Howling Wind

Here comes the angry wind
Lashing! Lashing! Against long blinds
Singing! Singing! The wailing song
And smashing the bare trees

Here comes the angry wind
Blowing! Blowing! A long whistle
Blaring its loud horn
And breaking every thistle

Mitzie Williams

Rain

Rain! Rain! All day
Drizzling from the sky
Seeping over the ragged mountains
Gushing over zig-zag terrains

Pitter! Patter! Over the scorched plains
Stumbling across sharp rocks
Cracking the dry soil
Trailing along the rivers into the sea
As thunder echoes down the valley.

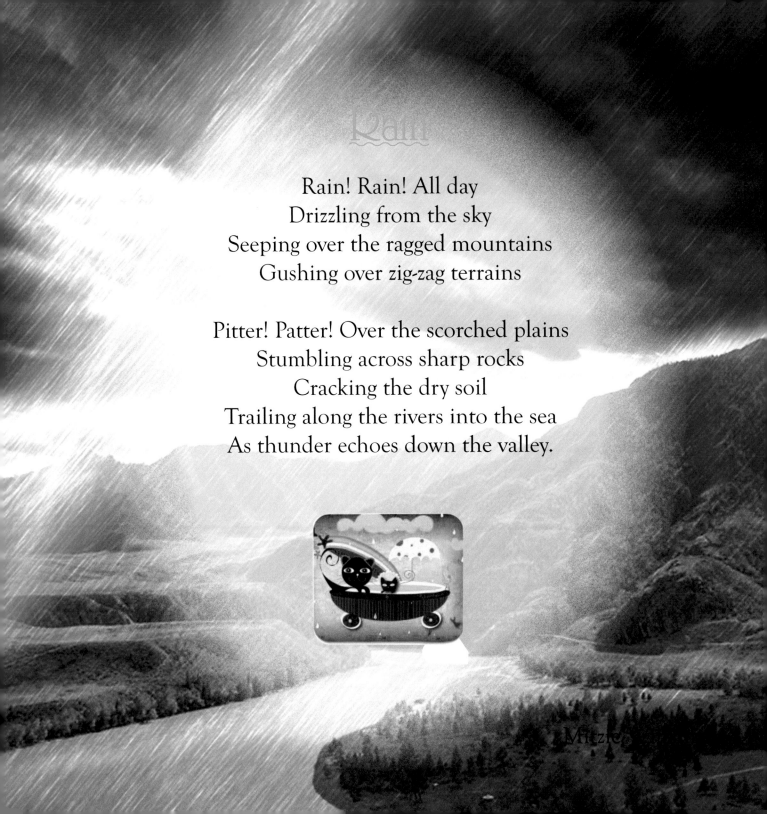

Mitzie

The Ship

Rolling! Rolling! On the
wide ocean
Comes the big ship
That goes on a long trip
Across the blue waters

Sailing! Sailing! Over the
splashing waves
Towards the pretty shore
Away from the hidden caves
The captain anchors the big ship

Mitzie Williams

Who Am I

I am a good boy
I am a good girl
I am a child of destiny

I am flesh
I am soul
I am spirit

With a great mind
Woven from my father
With threads from my mother
But, I am a child of destiny.

Mitzie Williams

Bedtime Stories

Joseph's Coat

Joseph was a very young boy. His parents were Jacob and Rachel. He was the youngest son of Jacob and Rachel. He had ten older brothers. He was a loving and caring boy. He looked after the sheep in the pasture. He wore a multi-colored coat that was a gift from Jacob. Joseph's coat was as pretty as a garden of flowers.

Joseph had many dreams and visions. He told his father about his puzzling dreams. Soon his brothers became very jealous of his dreams. They envied him and plotted to kill him. He had special dreams. In one dream he saw his brothers' sheaves of grain bow down before his own sheaves of wheat.

One day his wicked brothers decided to kill him. They tied him up and left him in a pit for many days. However, they changed their minds and sold him to a group of slave traders. They told Jacob that Joseph had been killed by a wild animal. Jacob missed Joseph and his dreams.

In the meantime, Joseph had been sold to Potiphar, a governor in Egypt. Soon Joseph was dreaming big dreams again. One day he was thrown in jail because he refused to sleep with Potiphar's wife. Joseph wanted to please God instead and do the right thing, but Potiphar's wife was very displeased. She had him thrown into jail.

Joseph was promoted to chief warden in the prison and was responsible for the other prisoners. One day, he interpreted a dream for a baker and a cupbearer. Joseph's interpretation of the dreams came through because the baker was killed while the cupbearer was set free.

One day, Pharaoh had an awful dream and none of his magicians or wizards could interpret it for him. The cupbearer remembered Joseph's interpretation of his dream and told Pharaoh. Pharaoh sent for Joseph and Joseph explained the meaning of the dream to him. Pharaoh was pleased and promoted Joseph as the chief governor in Egypt. Joseph was a good steward.

Just as Joseph said, in seven years time, famine spread throughout the land. Egypt was the only country with food and so Joseph's brother's came to buy food from Egypt. Joseph recognized his brothers, but they did not recognize him. Joseph sold them the food but made one special request. He asked that they bring Benjamin with them next time. When they brought Benjamin to Egypt, Joseph forgave them and invited his father and all his relatives to live in Egypt with him. He treated them well and gave them many lands for their sheep.

Joseph had become prosperous. Pharaoh was pleased with Joseph's leadership over Egypt. Joseph loved God very much. God provided him with a wife and two children. Joseph was helpful, kind, and wise. God gave him a special gift of dreams, visions, and interpretations.

Prayer

Dear Jesus, thank you for the gift of dreams and visions. Help me to understand my dreams. Help me to overcome the spirit of envy and jealousy. Help me to guard my dreams. Help me to follow my dreams. Guide me to fulfill my destiny.

Moral

The moral of this story is that you should guard your dreams with hope and courage and believe in your dreams.

Queen Esther's Wish

Esther was a good Jewish girl. She was also an orphan. Her uncle Mordecai raised her up to be a God-fearing woman. One day, the king began to search for a new wife and chose Esther. Esther became one of the many wives and concubines living in the palace.

Esther had a palace enemy whose name was Haman. He was very unkind and envious of Mordecai and plotted in secret against the Jews. He wanted to kill all the Jews. Haman tricked the King into signing a letter that ordered all the Jews to be killed. However, Mordecai found out about his secret plot. He begged Esther to help save the Jews.

Esther declared a three day fast for all the Jewish people. She knelt in prayer and sackcloth seeking God's help from Haman's plot. After three days of fasting, Esther went to see the King. There was a special rule that no one could enter into the King's presence unless, he stretched out his scepter towards them. Nevertheless, Esther was brave and confident enough to speak to the King. Then she entered his husband's chamber.

The King sat on his throne and stretched out his scepter to Queen Esther. She bowed before the King. She told him that she wanted him to attend a banquet with all the members of the palace staff. The King agreed to come to the banquet. She told Mordecai and sent out special invitations for everyone who worked in the palace to attend the great banquet feast. Meanwhile, Haman set up secret gallows to hang Mordecai on at the courtyard in his house.

Queen Esther prepared an enormous banquet with plenty of food to eat and drink. When everyone had eaten, Queen Esther requested that the King come to another banquet with Haman as the guest of honor. At the second banquet, Queen Esther asked Haman to stand up in front of the King. Then Esther told the King about the secret plot that Haman had to kill all of the Jews. She told the King that she was a Jew. The King was very, very angry. He asked Haman if Queen Esther's accusations were true. He stared at the King in terror and said "Yes, I am guilty but please spare my life because I did not mean to harm Esther or her people". Of course, Haman was lying because he did mean to harm them. He had wanted to kill every Jew in the city. So the King ordered that Haman and his entire family be hung on the same gallows he had prepared for Mordecai.

Moral

The King loved Queen Esther even more after this because she had been so brave. He gave her great honor and favor. Many people respected her because of the great faith and courage that she used to save her people. We should always pray and fast to meet our most difficult needs.

Prayer

Dear God,

Grant me a spirit, O God, like Esther's to believe that you will give me favor for any impossible situation. Like Esther, I am asking you to take the seal of destruction off my destiny. Destroy every yoke, bondage, and burden. Lord Jesus grant special favor and protection upon every family member and believer.

Amen.

Samuel Obeys

A long time ago there was a boy of eight years old, named Samuel. He was a good boy. His parents' names were Elkanah and Hannah. Before Samuel was born, Hannah prayed for a very long time to have a child. She made a vow to God that if God  blessed her with a child, she would return that child to God. God answered her prayers and Samuel was born.

When he was old enough, his mother gave him to Eli, the high priest at God's temple. Eli trained him to be a helper in the temple. Each year his mother came to visit him. She carried with her a new tunic made just for him.

One night, while Samuel was in a deep sleep, he was awakened by a strange voice calling, "Samuel! Samuel!" He stared out into the darkness but saw no one. Then he went to Eli and asked if he had called him but Eli said "No, go back to sleep Samuel." Samuel went back to sleep but was awoken a second time by the same whispering voice "Samuel, Samuel!" He went back to Eli who denied calling him and sent him back to bed again. When the same thing happened a third time, Eli realized that God must be calling Samuel. So he told him the next time he heard the voice to answer by saying, "Here I am Lord, use me Lord!"

The voice called Samuel for the fourth time and this time Samuel knew just what to do. He answered loudly and clearly "Hear I am Lord, use me Lord!" So the Lord spoke to Samuel that night and told him a great many things that would happen in the future!

Moral

We should always recognize God's voice. If unsure of whose voice it is, we should pray and seek help from parents, elders, pastors, or a spiritual counselors. Always seek wise advice and counseling for troubling issues and concerns. Samuel was anointed a prophet by God and he had learned to obey God's voice.

Prayer

Dear Heavenly Father,
Bless me with the spirit of obedience to my parents, teachers, pastors, and other people in authority. Help me to be a good listener. Help me to be humble, respectful, and to follow good advice. Help me to please ask for direction when I am not sure about something or someone. Thank you for leading me to be a better person.
Amen.

The Eagle's Eyes
A General Book of Poems
(94 pages)

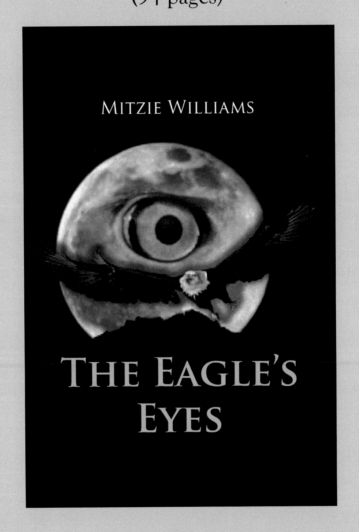

www.xlibris.com
E-mail: mitziewilliams89@yahoo.com

Printed in the United States
By Bookmasters